The Gingerbread Man

Picture words

cow

fox

gingerbread man

4

oven

tail

little old
woman

horse

One day, a little
old woman made a
gingerbread man.

She cooked him in
her oven.

The little old woman took
the gingerbread man from
the oven.

He jumped from her
hands and ran from
the house.

"Stop, little gingerbread man!" said the little old woman. "I want to eat you."

But the gingerbread
man did not stop.
He ran and ran.

The little old woman
ran too, but she did
not catch him.

Soon, the gingerbread man met a cow.

"Stop, little gingerbread man!" said the cow. "I want to eat you."

But the gingerbread
man did not stop.
He ran and ran.

The cow ran too, but
she did not catch him.

17

Soon, the gingerbread
man met a horse.

"Stop, little gingerbread
man!" said the horse.
"I want to eat you."

But the gingerbread
man did not stop.
He ran and ran.

The horse ran too, but
he did not catch him.

Soon, the gingerbread
man came to a river.
He met a fox there.

"I must cross the river,"
said the gingerbread man.

"Jump on my tail,"
said the fox.

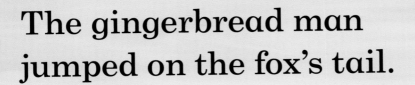

The gingerbread man
jumped on the fox's tail.

"My feet are in the water,"
said the gingerbread man.

"Jump on my back,"
said the fox.

24

The gingerbread man jumped on the fox's back.

"My feet are in the water," said the gingerbread man again.

"Jump on my head," said the fox.

The gingerbread man jumped on the fox's head.

"I'm hungry!" said the fox.

And he ate the gingerbread man!

29

Activities

The key below describes the skills practiced in each activity.

Spelling and writing

Reading

Speaking

Critical thinking

Preparation for the Cambridge Young Learners Exams

Look and read.
Put a ✓ **or a** ✗ **in the box.**

1  This is the old woman. ✓

2  This is the gingerbread man. ▢

3  This is the oven. ▢

4  This is the horse. ▢

5  This is the cow. ▢

2 **Look and read.**
Write yes or no.

"Stop, little gingerbread man!" said the little old woman. "I want to eat you."

11

1 The old woman baked the gingerbread man in her oven.

........yes........

2 The gingerbread man walked from the house.

3 "Stop!" said the old woman. "I want to drink you."

3 **Work with a friend.**
Talk about the two pictures.
How are they different?

a

But the gingerbread
man did not stop.
He ran and ran.

The cow ran too, but
she did not catch him.

b

But the gingerbread
man did not stop.
He ran and ran.

The horse ran too, but
he did not catch him.

Example:

In picture a,
there is one
animal.

In picture b,
there are two
animals.

4 Look and read.
Write *yes* or *no*. 📖 ✏️ ✴️

The gingerbread man jumped on the fox's tail.

"My feet are in the water," said the gingerbread man.

"Jump on my back," said the fox.

1 The little old woman is standing next to the horse. ....no.............

2 The gingerbread man is standing on the fox's back. ....

3 The fox is swimming in the river. ....

4 The gingerbread man's feet are in the water. ....

5 Find the words.

e	a	t	o	h	g
n	x	u	y	o	i
o	f	o	x	r	n
r	z	n	k	s	g
c	w	i	q	e	e
o	v	e	n	h	r
w	z	q	w	m	b
s	o	u	k	w	r
c	a	t	c	h	e
s	n	c	r	o	a
t	a	i	l	w	d

eat

catch

cow

fox

gingerbread

horse

oven

tail

6 Look and read.
Write the answers.

But the gingerbread man did not stop. He ran and ran.

The little old woman ran too, but she did not catch him.

1 Who has to run very quickly?

The little old woman has

to run very quickly.

2 Who cannot catch the gingerbread man?

....

....

3 What must the gingerbread man do?

....

....

36

7 **Look at the pictures.**
Tell the story to your teacher. 💬

Example:

> A little old woman made a gingerbread man . . .

8 Look at the pictures. One picture is different. How is it different? Tell your teacher. 💬 ❓

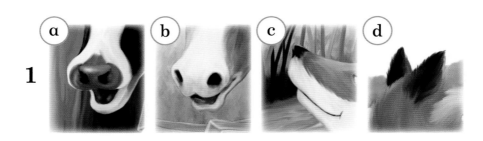

Picture d is different because it shows ears, not a nose.

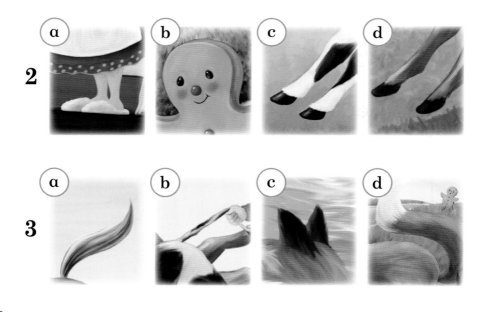

9 **Circle the correct sentence.**

1 The gingerbread man jumped from the oven and

    a he ran from the house.

    b he met a cow.

2 The gingerbread man did not stop and

    a the old woman sat down.

    b the old woman ran and ran.

3 The cow saw the gingerbread man and said,

    a "I want to play with you."

    b "I want to eat you."

4 The horse wanted to eat the gingerbread man but

    a the gingerbread man ran and ran.

    b the horse met a cow.

10 **Look at the picture and read the questions. Write the answers.** 📖 ✏️

The gingerbread man jumped on the fox's back.

"My feet are in the water," said the gingerbread man again.

"Jump on my head," said the fox.

1 Why didn't the fox say, "I want to eat you"? **(clever)**

Because he was clever.

2 Why did the gingerbread man jump on the fox's back? **(feet / in the water)**

3 Why did the fox eat the gingerbread man? **(hungry)**

11 **Ask and answer the questions about the picture with a friend.**

"Stop, little gingerbread man!" said the little old woman. "I want to eat you."

11

1 Does the old woman live in a city?

No, she does not.

2 What is the old woman doing? Why?

3 Why did she make the gingerbread man?

4 Why did the gingerbread man run from the house?

12 **Circle the correct picture.**

1 Who did not have any friends in the story?

a    b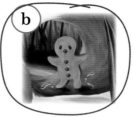

2 Who always eats grass?

a    b

3 Who sometimes cooks gingerbread men?

a    b

4 Who ate the gingerbread man?

a    b

13 **Write *on*, *behind*, or *in front of*.**

1 The little old woman ran

 __behind__ the gingerbread man.

2 The gingerbread man ran

 _____ the little old woman.

3 The cow and the horse ran

 _____ the gingerbread man.

4 The gingerbread man jumped

 _____ the fox's back.

5 The gingerbread man jumped

 _____ the fox's head,

and the fox ate him.

14 **Ask and answer questions about the picture with a friend.**

The gingerbread man jumped on the fox's head.

"I'm hungry!" said the fox.

And he ate the gingerbread man!

28

29

Example:

> Which animal did the gingerbread man meet first?

> He met the cow first.

15 Look at the picture.
Write short answers.

"Stop, little gingerbread man!" said the little old woman. "I want to eat you."

1 Did the little old woman think, "My gingerbread man can run very fast!"?

No, she did not.

2 Did the gingerbread man think, "She cannot catch me!"?

_____

3 Did the old woman think, "I can catch the gingerbread man!"?

_____

16 **Look and read. Write the correct words on the lines.** 📖 ✏️

cow   fox   oven   river

1 Which animal
eats grass and
gives us milk?   cow

2 Which animal
has a red and
white tail?   ....

3 Which one is
very hot?   ....

4 Which one is cold?   ....

17 **Ask and answer the questions with a friend.**

1 *What is your favorite animal? Why?*

My favorite animal is a dog because it is friendly.

2 Have you got any animals at home?

3 Would you like to have a horse or a cow? Why?

4 Do you sometimes see foxes?

Level 2

The Gingerbread Man

978–0–241–25442–4 ☐

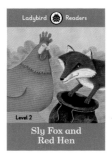

Sly Fox and Red Hen

978–0–241–25443–1 ☐

The Monster Next Door

978–0–241–25444–8 ☐

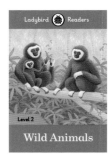

Wild Animals

978–0–241–25445–5 ☐

Little Red Riding Hood

978–0–241–25446–2 ☐

Dinosaurs

978–0–241–25447–9 ☐

Topsy and Tim The Big Race

978–0–241–25448–6 ☐

Peter Rabbit Goes to the Treehouse

978–0–241–25449–3 ☐

Sports Day

978–0–241–26222–1 ☐

Going on a Picnic

978–0–241–26221–4 ☐

Now you're ready for Level 3!

Notes
CEFR levels are based on guidelines set out in the Council of Europe's European Framework. Cambridge Young Learners English (YLE) Exams give a reliable indication of a child's progression in learning English.